A Day at the Seaside

A collection of short stories, poems and lyrics

Steve Shergold

First published in Great Britain 2020

Carraway Publishing

www.carrawaypublishing.co.uk

ISBN 978-1-9160950-0-7

Printed and bound in Great Britain by Clays Ltd, Elcograf S.p.A

A CIP catalogue record for this book is available from the British Library

For Jane, Sarah, Louise and Simon
and to all who follow after them

~

"Jim loves penguins" *Mum*

"Gatsby believed in the green light,
the orgastic future that year by year recedes
before us. It eluded us then but that's no matter
– tomorrow we will run faster, stretch out our
arms farther....And one fine morning –

So we beat on, boats against the current,
borne back ceaselessly into the past."

- *F. Scott Fitzgerald, The Great Gatsby*

Contents

Short Stories

A Day at the Seaside

1

The beach looked so still, there was no wind, the sea lapped gently along the shore. A few walkers were exercising their dogs who chased the waves, yelping with naive surprise as the sea bit them back causing a mist of spray over their owners as they shook themselves dry. Balls of all shapes and sizes were kicked and thrown by children who shrieked with delight, free for a few hours from the shackles of domestic and classroom confinement.

How different it was sixty years ago, thought

Gerald, as he stood watching this scene of peace and tranquility. He started to brush the hair from his eyes and then with a wry smile stopped, and drew in a deep breath, causing the button on his tunic to pop open, 'yes so different'.

The stench of cordite, shit, puke and death invaded his nostrils as he remembered his escape from the landing craft after over twelve hours at sea. Deafened by the noise of the shells and terrified of drowning he recalled the desperation he felt as he ran from one life-threatening situation towards the next, the German guns that were possibly seconds away from killing him. He was nineteen, with a light dusting of downy hair on his cheeks, he was still a virgin and he was going to win the war for Britain.

The 'umpa,' 'umpa' sound from behind broke him from his thoughts and made him turn around. A brass band was warming up,

their black and red waistcoats contrasting with
the multi-coloured bunting, representing all
the flags of the Allied Forces stretching the
entire length of the promenade. Halfway along
they exploded into full sized flags hung around
a temporary wooden stage which had been
erected for the great and the good to make
speeches later in the day. The German flag,
he noticed, was not present in this menagerie;
on this day sixty years ago over four thousand
men died on the beaches of Normandy,
twelve thousand in total before all the beaches
were secure. Men from over twenty different
nations fighting on both sides; the Diamond
anniversary, however, would be celebrated only
by the victors.

2

Gerald's war began on his eighteenth birthday
in 1943. He could not wait to join up, like many

boys of that age who had not yet discovered their own mortality he still had that belief of invincibility; that principle attribute of youth that Generals depend upon when sending young men into battle. At one stage he was terrified that it would be all over before he could, as he believed 'make a difference'. He never wanted to be anything else other than a soldier; such was the fate of his generation.

His parents made sure he was as well-educated as he could be on the income his father received as a manager at the local tyre factory. They had dreams for him of course, they thought he might be the first in their family to go to university, but being an accountant or a lawyer or pursuing any normal profession just seemed impossible in a nation that had yet to secure its own future. For any young boy growing up in a war, what else would or could they be.

Gerald thought nothing of this as he travelled to Wiltshire for his initial training. It was death or glory, medals and fighting, fighting, fighting that he was thinking of. The hissing of brakes on the green Leyland bus woke him from this reverie, as it arrived at Corsham barracks. He smiled to himself as he stepped down.

"Oi you scruffy little erk! Get over there in line with the others and take that stupid grin off your face or I'll take it off for you."

Corporal Stewart, standing tall and making the most of his five foot seven inches, looked immaculate. The crease in his trousers was sharp enough to peel the mess hall's potatoes, and the brogue on his shoes was so bright it was as if two dark mirrors were stood side by side competing in a reflection contest.

"Bloody hell," thought Gerald, "what a jumped-up little git."

Yet Corporal Stewart was anything but. At nineteen he was a fresh-faced recruit in the 'class of 39' part of the British expeditionary force, who were humiliated at the pyrrhic 'victory' at Dunkirk. Most of his fellow conscripts lay dead in the fields of France, but he was 'lucky' enough to survive to fight again with Montgomery at El Alemain and then in the liberation of Italy. Now at just twenty-three, the detached look behind his eyes told the keen observer something else; he knew where these boys were going, and he knew how few would come back.

Gerald stood in line behind a tall thin lad wearing a dark brown gabardine coat, loosely fitting trousers held up by a snake belt and blue jumper. He looked nervous and frightened.

"I'm Gerald," he said introducing himself quietly so as not to incur the wrath of the Corporal.

"Hello, I'm Tom and this is Jim," he responded, with a glance across to the boy on his left, who was fidgeting, and shifting from one foot to the other.

"Gerald or Jerry, ha, ha, he's a bloody Jerry," Jim replied with a nervous laugh in an attempt to impress the whole line, "so you're the one we'll be fighting eh, you don't look so tough." All the other recruits suppressed a laugh.

"Shut it you lot." came the terse reply from the Corporal.

Gerald grimaced; the last thing he wanted to be called was Jerry. The name however stuck and harmless as this joke was, it was the first chink in Gerald's illusion of personal invincibility.

Jim, as it turned out, was the joker in the pack. His Father was a butcher from Guildford and he had inherited his easy going nature, wit and the good humour which comes from a lifetime of flirting with housewives, serving up brisket and chopped liver in his shop. Jim loved attention and would go to any lengths to achieve it unlike Tom who was most happy with his head buried in a book, never speaking unless he was spoken to. Tom was also a chain smoker, lighting one Players unfiltered from the butt of the previous one. He trained to be an electrician before the war and had a fascination with everything electrical; within five minutes of selecting his bunk he had described, to all who would listen, the electrical wiring circuit of the barrack room.

"How bloody dull are you?" quipped Jim, "Why they call you electrical bods Sparky I'll never know." as he planted his fourteen stone frame onto the bunk above Tom's.

"Are you gonna tell me that chopping up some pig's trotter is any more interesting?"

said Gerald jumping to Tom's defence, whilst securing the next bed with his suitcase.

"I tell you what, in a few weeks' time you'll be gagging for boiled trotter, nothing better." Jim replied smacking his lips together in an exaggerated way and salivating at the same time.

As the banter developed, Jim became 'Trotter', Gerald, 'Jerry' and Tom, 'Sparky'; the irony of Tom's moniker was of course completely lost on him.

Over the next six weeks their friendships developed as they undertook their basic training. Corporal Stewart had the task of breaking all the new recruits from school boys into homogenous fighting machines with a single focus; to kill Germans. Once the initial training was completed, they were shipped down to a temporary billet near Slapton Sands in Devon where they joined thousands of other troops from all over the British Empire.

But mostly they were all "bloody yanks" as Jim described them. The training was intensive, disorganized and deadly. In one incident alone Jerry watched helplessly from the beach as several hundred of Jim's 'yanks' were killed when a U-boat attacked a landing craft that was practising an assault. Throughout it all however, the three chums stuck together cementing a bond between them that would last a lifetime; how long that lifetime would last none of them knew.

Finally, on the fifth of June 1944, after many false starts the call came to board the landing crafts for France. This time it was not a drill, 'Operation Overlord' had begun.

"Brought your trunks?" quipped Trotter as he lugged his Lee-Enfield 303 rifle up the gangway to the deck.

"I'd rather have a deck chair or better still a camp bed, we're gonna be on our feet for hours," replied Jerry, "I'm glad we got some chow down us beforehand."

"You won't be saying that when we're in the middle of channel." groaned Trotter.

All the time Sparky just stood with a cigarette in his mouth, studying the hydraulic system that would keep the door closed, the troops in and the sea out.

3

As the craft neared the French coast the three were in no shape to start liberating a country as the smell of diesel, sea water, sweat and the swell of the long crossing was beginning to take its toll. Jerry gulped down another breath of sea air desperately trying to suppress the bile that was forming in his stomach, "I can't wait to get off this boat," was all he could think when he felt a slight splash on his cheek, "bloody seagull" he said as he wiped the warm sticky mess away with his hand, and then he froze. "Why is this shit red?"

Time and motion stood still as his brain slowly struggled with the concept. Like a sledgehammer it dawned on him. Blood. He quickly checked himself, he seemed OK, and then looking around him, he saw Corporal Stewart lying with half his head missing, and then all hell let loose.

"Bang! Bang! Bang! Bang!" The explosion of shells shattered the silence. Both inside and outside his head the sound invaded his whole being. The boat went into panic.

An officer cried out, "Prepare to attack." The sea gate on the craft started to open, but the boat was still too far out and the sea gushed in like a tsunami. In the cacophony of the bombardment some of the men just stood rigid in their own personal silence, they became young boys again, a chap Jerry was friendly with during training urinated into his trousers, another cried out for his mum.

"Get off the frigging boat, before you all drown." shouted the Captain.

Jerry quickly came to his senses and grabbed Trotter and Jim and jumped, just as a shell exploded vaporizing three fellow liberators. The sea was no escape. Each man carried over 30 pounds of kit. When they hit the water they sunk; on tiptoe they could just about keep their heads out of the water. Jerry's first taste of battle was a mouth of salty water. Swallowing half of it he choked violently evacuating both his lungs and the remains in his stomach at the same time.

The German bullets raked into the sea forcing many to seek sanctuary under water or turn back to the boats, but as the sea turned red there was no place to hide. The three edged their way towards the shore, shrapnel whistled around them, along with short stifled screams of men who had trained for weeks, but were destined to be nothing more than bullet stoppers, buying time for the lucky ones to reach the beach.

"Jim are you OK?" Jerry called out.

"Shit! All me bloody fags are wet." gasped Sparky in reply.

"Now he has a sense of humour." murmured Trotter.

"I don't think he's joking." Jerry spluttered as he focused his attention on the patch of yellow sand ahead of him.

They dragged themselves onward towards the beach and the German guns. Then, as Jerry stepped out of the water onto the beach, "Pop." like a fuse blowing at a floodlit football match: darkness.

4

The orange coach had "Stones of Bath" stencilled down one side as it pulled up on the promenade in a long line of similar vehicles bearing the names of their home towns, 'Grants of Grimsby', 'Bob's Coaches, Birmingham' and others from Cardiff, Edinburgh and everywhere else in the UK it seemed.

Sixty years on this was a gentler invasion with colour TV, air conditioning and waitress service, the only bombardment their occupants received were kisses from the local French welcoming party. One by one they disembarked, all dressed in uniform, in regimental ties, a beret neatly positioned on their heads, grey slacks and of course a blue blazer boasting a chest full of ribbons and medals that glinted in the June sun.

They were much older now of course, most were in their eighties, many like Sparky needed a wheelchair brought around to the steps of the bus. Trotter, didn't though, "Fit as a butcher's dog." he would snort, over and over again to anyone who would listen. A nurse in a crisp white habit helped Sparky settle into his chair; he had already lit up a cigarette, desperate for a nicotine fix after the five hours curfew on the coach. Seventy-nine years old and neither the war nor the fags has finished him off mused Jerry as he looked on.

Watching the old soldiers gather he thought to himself, this anniversary will be the last that we will all attend together. Few will be alive for the seventieth and if they are their health will make the journey impossible. As each year passes a few less will return until one day no one will come and remember this great battle. The memories will fade with each generation and finally D-day will be consigned to the graveyard of history books, just a memorial plaque on the beach wall. There will be no more old soldiers to tell the tale, no more pomp or ceremony, no more bunting, no more speeches by Presidents.

Jerry looked up. Sparky and Trotter were almost with him now. He waved. They wouldn't see him of course, they never did. He had stood on that beach every day for sixty years and would do so for all eternity, but today was special, it would be the last day he would stand here with his pals. After that it would be just another day at the seaside.

The Traveller

As many men of my vintage approaching their late fifties, I recently became overwhelmed by a sense of nostalgia. This was very strange for me, as I've never been too concerned about the past, rather I focus on the moment and then let everything else take care of itself. Too many people I'd seen in my work were consumed by it, so much so that their lives have been dominated either by living with the ghosts of their past or dealing constantly with the anxiety of a *make believe* future. Nevertheless, I'd now found myself with 'time on my hands' so I decided to give into this whim and visit the small market town where I grew up.

On a bright, crisp sunny Monday morning I parked my car next to my old scout hut, which surprisingly was still there, and even more unbelievable was still accommodating scouts. I started to wander up the high street. Much had changed, well after forty years, one would expect some change. However, I was more surprised by the places that hadn't, the old Liberal and Conservative clubs were pretty much as I remembered them, and most surprisingly 'The Toy Shop' was still exactly the same as it was throughout my whole time of living there. It had the same counter as it did in 1966, when I was buying Thunderbird Two or some other Gerry Anderson creation.

I smiled to myself, as after spending the last 25 years in marketing I just loved the fact that the original owner in the 1960s decided to call it 'The Toy Shop', no ambiguity. It says exactly what it sells. Toys.

My biggest joy however, was that the library was still there, exactly as I left it. Memories came flooding back, as I remember visiting every two weeks with my mum and sisters to change our books. Each visit bristled with excitement as each selection opened a door to a new world of adventure and escape.

Other places had changed. Woolworths had gone of course and so had Smiths, now an estate agent, and overall the high street had adopted the declining feel of many a small town whereby independent shops had now given over to charity shops and ubiquitous café chains.

I thought I would stop for a coffee at 'Farmer Giles' an old haunt of mine, where I would meet friends on a Saturday morning. It was gone of course, along with its Formica tables and its frothy coffee-flavoured milk, but in its place, there was still a café. So, in I went.

I cast my eye around for a table and ordered a flat white.

Sat on the table next to me was a lady of an indeterminate age, who seemed vaguely familiar. She was dressed in a stylish sixties black and yellow number, matched with uncomfortable looking high heeled shoes, which I must say, she carried off well. She looked like she had just stepped off the set of an Audrey Hepburn movie, minus of course, her signature long cigarette holder. She looked out of time and place for the twenty first century, but then I remembered everyone in this town was a sort of a misfit. I should know, I'm one myself.

My coffee arrived and I got out my diary to write up my thoughts, the lady looked across to me and said, "Are you a traveller?"

I looked up and met her eye, I studied her for a few moments and replied, "Yes I have travelled, why do you ask?"

"I love to travel, it is my passion, I have seen, heard, tasted and smelt things that are beyond the imagination of most folk in this world.

"That's very interesting," I replied, "travel does broaden the mind" I winced as I bit hard on my cliché.

"Most people travel, like they live their lives, too busy planning or worrying about the next place they are going to, rather than experiencing where they are now on the journey; so actually, they have never been anywhere. People don't realise that time is an illusion, they ask what happened to the last, ten or even twenty years, not realising that for the most of that time their mind was somewhere else".

"Wow, that's really profound", I replied, "please tell me more."

She looked up at the ceiling, closed her eyes, and for a moment I thought she had gone into a trance. "Let me tell you about my visit to Istanbul. I immediately felt the history. Straddling the borders between East and West for over sixteen millennia, creating the famous Silk Road. The original city, Byzantium was a centre of civilisation six hundred and sixty years before the birth of Christ, bursting with art, music, science, which had adopted a wide cultural acceptance to people of all races and religions. All at the time, when back here in our little island we were wrapping ourselves in pig skin and trying our best to whack everyone in the next village over the head with a big stick."

I smiled, some sort of Sean Bean, Westeros, Game of Thrones image came to mind, but what she said was probably very true.

Still staring into space she continued her recollection, "I am there now. I can at this moment smell the fragrant herbs, purees, glistening olives all from the Inebolu, one of the oldest spice markets in the world. It satisfies yet terrifies every sense at the same time. They have every type of nut you can imagine, crates of bright colourful flowers that confuse the mind as you conceive everything that is both beautiful and ugly in a single moment."

"But if you go there, don't be put off by the grime, and the seedy looking tobacco chewing traders who eyeball every wanderer with such a deep perceived menace, which can, for the virgin visitor, send a primeval shudder down the spine that makes one want to turn and walk away as fast as possible. Cast off your Western prejudices and brave the walk. You will not be disappointed."

She stopped talking and gave me a long enquiring look that demanded a response. "I think I am beginning to understand, what you mean by enjoying each place and savouring each moment as it happens."

"Yes, the past is just a unique collection of memories, that only you can know, and the future is just a creation of your imagination. The present moment is all we have, but once experienced you can re-create it at any time. Yes, for example when I visited those beautiful islands in the Atlantic Ocean, the moment was overwhelming. Time stands still, the colours and smell of lilac and hydrangeas saturate my senses and I can almost taste the pollen as the bees create a mist of new life with every engagement."

"Yes, just being in the moment, losing all other distraction can be very enlightening", I replied, "what other places have you visited?"

"Many, many places, but I know that you also have travelled to different places, and different times." I felt a shiver go through my spine and gave her a curious look.

"Times?" I replied.

"Yes, I have watched over you all your life. I have seen you visit places both in the past and in the future. You have walked behind Cicero and watched as the Roman Republic fell, and then rise again like the Roman Empire. Your heart has been both broken and healed as you watched Dr. Urbino's love blossom and endure in the Time of Cholera. You laughed as you found your perfect soul mate in High Fidelity's anti-hero Rob Gordon....yes, the music probably did come before the misery; or was it the other way around?

You cried as you stood alongside Carton on the steps of the Guillotine, as he told the world, that today he will do, 'a far, far better thing than he has ever done before', and you, like Gatsby felt his pain as he reached out, but never quite touched the symbol of his hope; the green light at the end of Daisy's dock."

"Those books, you know about the books I

have read?" I sat up rigid, and stared at her, slightly spooked.

"Yes, and not just your top five", she winked and continued, "I know things about you, that no one else can know. Like me, you have read a thousand books, about a thousand places, in a thousand different times. We are much the same you and me; like you, I am a traveller, but I have never travelled. Not yet, not in the time that I am in now, but I will".

I stared down at my coffee, now very confused. I tried to gather my thoughts. Where was this going? I decided to go with it and mumbled a reply, "Yes, I agree, books can take you to places that trains and planes can never go, and good writers can create that moment in the mind's eye. You really believe you can hear, smell, touch and feel the place they are writing about but, just to be clear, are you saying you have never been to those places you described?"

There was no answer when I looked back, she had gone. Not a trace. I rushed outside and looked down the street. Was it my imagination or did I see her walk through the Library doors? I looked again but no one was there. Was she ever there? Was I so wrapped up in my own nostalgic moment, that I just imagined the last ten minutes, had I just seen a ghost?

I went back inside the café to pick up my jacket and diary. In the corner where she sat, I noticed something lying on the seat next to me. It was an old library ticket, the cardboard jacket type that you used before computers took over. I picked it up. The writing was faded, but I could just make out the date; June, nineteen sixty..something, it wasn't clear. The name was barely visible, I looked at it again. Finally, I understood. I understood everything.

I went outside, and looked back at the library,

I looked again at the ticket. It had finally come home. I knew then, at that moment, that one bright sunny morning I would follow her through those doors. We would meet again.

The Traveller

A Day at the Seaside

Dum tee Dum tee Dum

I used to work with a guy, Tony was his name, and he was the bass player in a band. I was not impressed. Bass players, I thought, were very dull, they just stood at the back of the stage playing 'dum tee dum tee dum'. It looked dead easy and rather pointless. If you were going to be in a band, you'd better be the lead singer or guitarist, or, at the very least the keyboard player, not the bass player.

Anyway at the time being in a band held no interest, for me, what mattered was scoring a goal for the local fourth division factory team that was rooted to the bottom of the District League. We played a liberally expansive game without any hope of promotion or fear of relegation, because at this level of football there was nowhere to be relegated to. But this did not matter, in this town, at this age you played football, therefore, football was my life.

Then one day Tony invited me to one of his gigs in a nearby City. I was only eighteen and he was in his mid-twenties, I was flattered that he should ask me and, that by saying 'Yes I'll come' I would also impress him as well. So I picked up my girlfriend and we drove to the venue. Tony played in a blues combo called 'Dean Gabber and Gabberdeans'. I loved the name, and in the car on the thirty mile trip we played games making up other fictional band names, 'Mac Plastic and the Plastic Macs' was one of the better ones we came up with; we were out for a laugh, nothing more.

We entered the pub, through a fug of stale beer and tobacco. I ordered a pint of Butcombe bitter and a coke for my girlfriend and we waited for the music to begin. I had very little interest in music and had seen very few bands, my expectation for the evening was low.

Dean came onto the beer-stained stage, dressed in, surprise, surprise, a dirty old raincoat and dark sunglasses. He grabbed the microphone, insulted the audience, and then his gravelly voice exploded into a cover of 'Friday on my mind' by the Easybeats, followed by a string of standards such as 'Jonny B Good' and 'Brown Sugar'. But I heard very little of this. My eyes were transfixed on Tony and his guitar. He did not just play his bass, he attacked it, caressed it, slapped it, at times he appeared to make love to it. His performance was far more than just playing a plank of wood with four strings on it, it had passion and soul; he stared passed the audience with the empty eyes of a junkie; lost in the music.

That evening changed my life. The next day I went and begged for a loan from my bank and bought an electric bass guitar. It completely consumed me, I practised every day for hours on end. I got up at six every morning so I could practise an hour before I went to work. I practised and practised. I screamed at myself when I could not master a technique. I practised and practised. The calluses on my fingers cracked and bled. I practised and practised. When a record played on the radio, I heard only the bass line. I practised and practised.

I moved to the City and joined a band. We played 80's post punk rock, a style at the time known as new wave. We wrote our own songs, we fly-posted, we supported some leading local bands, and on one occasion we played with a band that had a hit played on 'Top of the Pops'. We were even interviewed on the radio by Johnny Walker.

I stretched my learning further, I learnt all the scales not just the major and the minor, but the Blues, the Ionian, Dorian, Phrygian, Lydian, Mixolydian, Aeolian and Locrian. The different playing styles, the pop, the slap, the hammer-on, finger style, pick and soloing. I gained respect from other musicians, other bands asked me to play for them.

I was still in close touch with my old pals and occasionally I went to watch them play the odd football match, but they never came to see me play; ever. I was a little upset by this and asked one of them why, he replied, "Well, what's the big deal, you're just the bass player, you stand at the back, playing dum tee dum tee dum."

The Letter

It was a bright clear, but very cold day, the temperature was hovering around zero, and I turned the collar of my coat up around my ears to protect them from the chill of a slight breeze. I ordered coffee as I sat in Groben square, my false hip smarting as if the cold had impaled itself deep into my bones.

I was waiting for an old friend of mine, a man I had known for over forty years. Each week we played chess and each week we talked and talked about the 'old days'. I saw him approach, stooping and slightly losing his balance as he tried to avoid a young boy on a skate board. I rose from my seat to greet him.

"Hello my friend." I announced as we gave each other our customary hug.

"Sergio." he replied, "Did you get my letter?"

"Slow down, relax, drink some coffee, there is plenty of time before we start putting the world to rights."

"Sergio", he replied "After forty years of speculation, we finally have a chance to find out the truth. I do not want to go to my grave without knowing the bastard that betrayed us."

I looked at him for a moment, he was dressed like me in grey from head to foot, grey flannel trousers, grey shirt, and a grey coat. His short grey hair, which still covered most of his head was cut in a sharp military style and his thick tortoiseshell rimmed glasses were perched on a small but very straight nose. To everyone else in that square we were invisible, two old men whose time had passed, playing out their final years.

As I watched him I reflected on the cause of his excitement. Earlier in the week I had noticed, on the door mat of my small flat, the type afforded to all retired employees of the local pharmaceutical factory, a letter. It stood apart from the dull brown cheap Government correspondence that normally littered my hallway. As I picked it up I immediately recognised the delicate, yet crafted handwriting; it was from my old friend Joseph. A shiver ran through my spine as I opened it. I was perplexed, Joseph would never write to me, I play chess with him every week, what would be the point? I unfolded the heavy paper and as I read, my blood froze and my mind returned in the blink of an eye, to a damp autumn morning at the State University, nearly half a century ago.

~

"Come this way, come this way," fussed a small bald headed man in pin-striped trousers and round rim-wired glasses, "all new students are to register in the refectory. Please ensure you have your official documentation ready." I looked at the scene in front of me, a large wooden doorway leading into a red bricked hall, built in the seventeenth century. Once it would have been magnificent, but now neglected by the new regime, it looked tired and patched up like an old actress clinging onto her former beauty.

Through this portal passed a stream of young men dressed identically in charcoal suits, heavy coats and all carrying sturdy, worn, brown leather suitcases that looked as if they had been passed down from father to son. "The lucky ones", I thought, that was what we were told by everyone we met, the privileged few who, because we either knew someone, or we had parents who had bribed the entrance officials with their life savings or, like me, had won one of the few scholarships available, had the chance to escape what would certainly be a lifetime of hard labour, either in the fields or the factory.

"Hello, I was just looking at your luggage label, are you from Rostov?" called out a voice from behind me.

I looked around to see a boy of my age, with hope beaming from his bright blue eyes.

"My name's Joseph, I'm from Rostov province too," he continued, "I live in a small village, five miles south of the capital."

"Yes I do, I am very pleased to meet you, my name is Sergio, and I think I know your village, it has the church with the steeple that leans to the left. Are you registering as well?" I replied.

"Yes, yes." he laughed, relief overwhelming

him like a spring tide on an empty beach. "I am so pleased to meet someone from my region; everyone I have met so far seems so aloof and unapproachable."

From this first meeting our friendship flourished. I subsequently learnt that Joseph's parents had died when he was young and that he had inherited everything they owned. Not much, but with the help of his aunt whose husband was a minor civil servant in the capital, it was enough to secure him a place at the University. I also learned that Joseph had political interests, a dangerous ambition in a country that was ironically described by its unelected leader as a democratic republic.

As the first term passed Joseph's interests in Agricultural Economics, the subject chosen for him to study, fell fallow in favour of this new passion. And he was not alone. He found many new friends sympathetic to his view that our country should be democratic in practice as well as in name. He started a secret college newspaper, 'The People's Voice', all the contributions were anonymous, but everyone including the college principals knew who had written them.

The officials however, treated Joseph and his group as harmless young men blowing off steam. As long as his activities were contained within the walls of the university, they knew they were in control, and more often than not, when faced with the stark reality of upsetting the authorities with radicalism or taking a comfortable job inside the system they were fighting, the latter always prevailed. But Joseph's activities had been noticed by someone else too.

~

A seagull squealed above my head and brought me sharply back to the present day and my meeting with Joseph in the square. He was clearly eager to speak.

"I spent five long years in a state prison because of this betrayal, I lost everything, and if it was not for you my dear friend, bringing food parcels every week I would have starved to death. You understand why this is so important to me?"

"Yes." I replied, "But we have had this conversation over and over again. You were set up, the fall guy in an operation that was out of your league. At the university you were an impressionable young man, you did not see it and the authorities knew this was their chance. Their spies were everywhere."

"Rubbish, it was not a spy, it was one of those tutors greedy for the reward money that grassed on me." countered Joseph, tightening his grip on his coffee cup.

At this point of the conversation Joseph lowered his eyes so that they would not meet mine. Was his conviction beginning to fade or did it mean something else? I thought back to the incident so many years ago that Joseph was referring to that was to change both our lives.

~

"Well, well look who's here, it's two of our local intelligentsia." said a softly spoken cultured voice, as Joseph and I drank a Vodka together to celebrate his twenty first birthday, "Come to drink amongst the stupid proletariat." he added.

I looked around and saw a tall thin man in his early thirties, dressed in a brown wool suit and who sucked on a Harlamov pipe. He had a ragged scar underneath his left eye which along with its partner studied us intently as he waited for a reply.

"No", responded Joseph quickly, "It's my birthday, and please don't mistake us for some of my fellow students. Sergio and I are not like them, we are country boys from Rostov."

As Joseph surveyed the man in front of him he added more slowly, "but surely sir, were you not a student once yourself?"

"No, no, I am just a simple administrator," said the stranger, "but I am very pleased to meet you two 'country' boys, and I'm glad our glorious Government has been so generous to send you to this esteemed seat of learning. My name is Victor, and Happy Birthday. Please let me refresh your glasses, Vodka isn't it?"

Young as we were, we both understood sarcasm when we heard it, yet this did not stop us from getting very drunk with our new friend. He was able to talk knowledgeably about every subject especially politics and I could see that as each hour passed, he was making a major impression on Joseph.

"What a grand comrade," Joseph burped as we left the bar and weaved our way down the narrow streets to our digs, "Did you listen to his ideas? He was really interested in the work I am doing to spread the word at college with the People's Voice."

"Yes, but you should be careful, our tutors may tolerate your political fantasies, but there are secret police everywhere and they take an entirely different view."

"These are not fantasies, Sergio. With more men like Victor we can change this country and create a world where everyone is free to make their own decisions and not just do what our Government tells them." he replied, too loudly for my liking.

"Keep quiet you idiot," I growled back through gritted teeth, all of a sudden very sober, "you will get us both arrested."

"Ok," he countered, "but you will see, he invited me to a meeting on Wednesday night."

"Just be careful, my friend, you may be getting in way over your head."

The following day Joseph chased me out of one of the lecture theatres, "Sergio slow down," he said excitedly, "let's go into the billiards room, it's normally quiet in there." We slipped unnoticed into the darkened room.

"I know who Victor is. I was right; he is one of us." Joseph whispered, even though there was no one around to hear us. "I have spoken to a few of the chaps who work on the newspaper and they are pretty sure that he is Victor Hayek, the leader of the PPFL."

"One of us." I laughed, "Is he a student? And what on earth is The PPFL?"

"He's the leader of The Peoples Party for

Freedom and Liberation, where have you been Sergio? You must know them?"

"This is crazy Joseph, your imagination is running riot and anyway we only know his first name. How can you be sure he is anyone other than a liberal hot-head who likes a drink?"

"My contacts say it must have been him. He is targeting editors of university newspapers to gather support for his movement amongst students and most significantly, he has a scar under one of his eyes, plus he was smoking that weird pipe; apparently a trademark of his."

Joseph's eyes narrowed as he continued, and his next words came out under his breath.

"And, remember he asked me to meet him in the old library building tomorrow at seven in the evening."

I suspected that prior to our encounter in the bar Joseph was as ignorant of Victor

Hayek and the PPFL as I was, but later that day I quietly asked around and was surprised to discover that it was possible that our erstwhile drinking partner could have been the notorious dissident.

Rumours about him were as diverse as they were wild, some said that he was a self-exiled foreigner from a neighbouring country where the death penalty awaited him on return, others claimed he was a direct descendent of the deposed Kaiser, desperate to reclaim his power and the throne.

Joseph's colleagues at the People's Voice claimed that the Government had invested a lot of time and energy suppressing any news of him. What they all agreed on was that he was the most wanted political activist in the country and a 10,000 Roubles reward awaited any citizen who could provide information that would lead to his arrest. A tempting offer,

I thought, when the average annual income was less than a third of this amount.

~

"You know our old friend Levko who now works for our new Government?" Joseph's voice cutting through the icy air brought me back to our coffee and current discussion. The hairs on my back bristled as I listened to what he said next,

"Well as I alluded to in my letter, he says that he has come across a file that details the events that led up to Victor's capture and execution and my imprisonment. He says that although the names were changed to protect all informers, he is sure that I would know who the betrayer is from the profile described in the file. And he wants to meet me later today; Sergio this is our chance for revenge!"

I reflected that the new Government had

categorically stated that any collaborators from the old regime were still considered to be traitors and if caught would be tried, and if found guilty, forced to serve long prison sentences. I looked at him.

Discovering this new information had brought a glow to his otherwise wrinkled face. For a brief moment he looked just as he had in his youth before the scars of incarceration and old age had taken their toll. I took a deep breath, looked him full in the face and replied,

"Joseph, I beg you, let the past go, this could be a Pandora's Box, who knows what evils it could release."

I had tried to keep calm and measured as I delivered these words, but I noticed that instead I was pleading with him to drop the investigation; but I knew in my heart he would not.

"Are you crazy, Sergio? I have waited a lifetime to find out the answer to this question, you know I have my suspicions, and finally this will be the proof I need to nail our old tutor. So do you agree to come with me?"

I shuffled uncomfortably on the hard wooden seat. I became uncomfortably warm despite the cold weather, a hot sticky sweat started to run down my back.

As I had told myself countless times, Joseph would never understand, my parents lived in poverty; they had no food, no doctors, and when my mother fell sick there was no one in the village to help her. Money for proper medical care was needed desperately if she was to survive. I had needed that reward money

If only he had met me back at the bar after the meeting with Hayek as we agreed rather than staying for that extra drink. He would have escaped, I would have had the money; it should have been perfect. To hell with him, I thought, he has brought this on himself; I am too old for prison and redemption.

I broke away from my tortured thoughts, met his gaze, nodded and reluctantly conceded to his request, "Yes, Ok, if this is what you want, I will come to the meeting with you. Maybe you will find out the truth after all, but I have to go now, I will see you later. Goodbye my old friend."

As I left the table, I slipped a potassium cyanide tablet into Joseph's coffee cup, gave him a final wave and walked slowly across the square.

The Letter

A Day at the Seaside

Dave was good at football

Dave was good at football, he knew he was good at football, so he didn't bother at school. Why should he, he was good at football. From the age of nine he had been on Rovers books, "He showed promise, he could be a pro." they said.

So he left school with no qualifications. At sixteen Rovers signed him, only one of twenty boys who was offered a full-time contract. Dave was good at football, of the twenty, only two made it to the first team, Dave was one of them. Dave was good at football, and Rovers was only the beginning, the first step on the ladder. He was good at football, so for him surely the Premier League beckoned and England was in touching distance.

Although Dave was good at football, he never made it to the Premier League. He never made it to the Championship. In fact, whilst Dave was good at football, he was not quite good enough. Whilst Beckham earned ninety thousand a week at Real Madrid, Dave earned two thousand a week at Rovers.

A tidy sum, more than many of his old school mates, who although had qualifications were lucky to make £500 a week. He bought a house, a fast BMW and a Paul Smith suit, but he wasn't rich. He saved a little, but not much. He married the local beauty queen and she, believing he was David Beckham, spent like Posh Spice. What little he had, she spent, and when there was nothing left, she left.

After a career in the lower leagues playing for, Barnsley, Bradford, Burnley, and a loan period with Brentford, he finally ran out, not only of clubs beginning with B, but also any sort of contract. At the age of 32, he was on his own, unemployed and without any qualifications. In the pub his mates would say, "that's Dave, he used to be good at football."

George's last day

George stood in the dining room, a faded yellow duster in one hand and a plastic bottle of wood polish in the other. He was dressed impeccably in a black morning suit, with medium length tails, a crisp white shirt, black bow tie and white gloves. To protect his outfit from the dust and dirt of his occupation, a white apron was tied neatly at the back in a single bow. This last garment was unfortunate as George stood six foot tall, had strong square shoulders, a square jaw, and sharp piercing eyes, however the apron still made him look, as his master would often joke, like a slightly camp James Bond.

The room itself was decorated in the Regency

style; high ceilings, adorned with elaborate cornices, from which a glass chandelier hung so low it almost touched a magnificent silver punch bowl that formed the centre piece of an oak table that could seat over twenty guests. Velvet curtains fell across six windows, dividing the walls which were adorned with Italian frescos and more traditional paintings depicting scenes such as an old-fashioned English hunt with bulbous men dressed in red coats, bushy beards and cream jodhpurs, rearing up on black stallions.

On closer inspection, clues to the contemporary time George was living in were everywhere in the room. There were ten flat micro speakers discretely built into the fake panelled walls, a green control panel glowed faintly by the door, and the tops of the brushed titanium window panels peeped out beneath the crushed velvet pelmet. Furthermore, if you listened very carefully you could hear the Higgs Phase Velocity Turbines or HPVTs as they were more commonly known, humming quietly from deep within the bowels of the spaceship.

George had worked as a butler for the Thomas family for as long as he could remember, in fact when the children were growing up they would ask him, "George, where did you come from before you started to work for mummy and daddy?". George would just defer and say, "Oh, I don't know it seems to me that I've always worked for your parents". Lizzy was his favourite of the Thomas daughters, she seemed so much more perceptive and grown up than her other sisters. She recognised from an early age that there was more to George than just a feather duster.

She would ask him questions about the Earth and the universe it was suspended in. She wanted to know how many stars there were? Would the sun ever stop shining and how hot was it? And why can't humans breathe in space without a special suit? George always took the time to respond with simplified, yet considered and factual answers to these complex questions.

~

George did have a past. For over thirty years he had worked on NASA's top secret Omega drive programme, the system that would finally dispel Einstein's theory that nothing with mass could travel faster than the speed of light. Solving this problem would be akin to the development of the piston engine and jet engine in the nineteenth and twentieth centuries or the hydrogen engine in the twenty first century.

Throughout the entire twenty second century scientists had grappled with this problem, because even using the latest cold fusion nuclear power plants spacecraft could only travel at around one third of the speed of light.

Travelling around our own galaxy was a straightforward exercise, a trip to the Neptune barium mines, a distance of just over two and half billion miles from Earth, was a fourteen hour space flight and if you wanted to you could 'stop over' on one of the many transit hotels on Saturn. However, beyond our solar system the nearest star, Alpha Centauri, was over four light years away, so even at these speeds it would take more than twenty four years to get there and back. In many ways when George started work on the project, exploring outside our own solar system was as much a distant dream as it was when men first landed on the moon nearly three hundred years ago.

The problem was this, apart from electro-magnetic radiation such as light or radio waves anything with an intrinsic mass, a human being or a spaceship for example, is constrained by Einstein's special theory of relativity. In simple terms if you accelerated a spaceship towards the speed of light, it would become progressively smaller but its mass would exponentially increase; therefore to achieve constant acceleration it would require more and more energy to propel it.

A simple although not entirely accurate analogy would be to imagine an Olympic athlete trying to break the ten thousand metre world record. The gun sounds, he sprints away. As he completes the first lap an official hands him a twenty kilogram bag of potatoes, he draws on his internal energy reserves to compensate for the extra weight, but at the next lap the official hands him another twenty kilogram bag of potatoes and so on. After just a few laps the runner's energy is exhausted and he is so weighed down by the sacks of potatoes he can hardly move. Likewise as the spaceship approached the speed of the light both the energy required to continue accelerating and the mass the spaceship would attain in doing so would become infinite. In 'Earth' terms at this speed the spaceship would weigh the same as the entire universe that it was trying to fly around in.

A taxing conundrum indeed, however, the great contradiction that had intrigued George and his colleagues (and indeed scientists for over two hundred years) was that the restraints described by Einstein's special theory only *appear* to apply to objects we can see, touch and feel. Objects that are very, very small, comply with different laws known as Quantum Mechanics. Observations of this hypothesis showed that particles could move between two places instantaneously; both conjectures could not be correct. The Earth's resources had already run out and all the nearby planets had been well harvested. If mankind was to continue, new sources had to be found and found quickly, beyond our own galaxy. The world was pinning its hopes on a single unified theory that would allow this to happen.

George was put into a team headed up by Nobel Prize winning scientist Dr Simon Steel who by this time, in his late fifties, was considered 'old school', by many of his detractors. Rather than following accepted scientific dogma, he relied heavily on instinctive creativity and intuition to get results.

His appointment was therefore seen by many as a risk, but everyone, even his rivals, agreed he was a genius. He had developed in the past what many thought was impossible, an anti-gravitational device that allowed terrestrial vehicles to 'float' in designated 'air lots'. This had solved in an instant the parking and traffic congestion in major cities, whilst still allowing citizens the option of personal transport.

The challenge ahead of them was just as considerable. Not only was the team's remit to unify the two great, yet flawed theories of modern science they had to use the result to build a spacecraft that had the capability to cross entire galaxies in a single hop.

George was chosen because he had very special skills, he was able to compute complex numbers, very fast. Also he could perform these computations whilst simultaneously writing formula and projections that astrophysicists and engineers could use to modify prototype particle accelerators and matter-processing machines as they were working on them. This contribution was invaluable to Dr Steel as he was able to take George to committee meetings and perform live demonstrations of the progress being made, deflecting any political and budget concerns.

The two formed a close partnership. Dr. Steel was able to relate far more easily to George than other colleagues, relying heavily on his analytical powers to complement his own. With George, he was able to push to the very edge of the known scientific envelope, and then go off in an entirely different direction without the questioning and criticism that he often received from other members of the team. George just did what he was told; he took in the eminent Doctor's data and processed the results. Night after night they worked, the Doctor himself rarely going home, preferring to sleep on the floor of the laboratory. Hard work, of course never bothered George.

They tried everything, exploring all the current theories including, *anomalous dispensation* whereby it was thought that in certain circumstances atomic gases could travel faster than the speed of light; *pulsar theory* in which astrophysicists had observed that radio pulses from a pulsar could achieve superluminal speeds in space, and countless others. But they all proved fruitless.

Then one night after Steel had collapsed at his workstation through lack of sleep George continued his mission of researching past-over ideas when he came across a Portuguese physicist who had lived in Spain in the early part of the twenty first century. He had put forward the idea that in the very early days of the universe, light must have travelled faster than the accepted value. In fact, he stated that light could vary its speed up to sixty times faster than this figure.

Although he published his work termed 'The varying speed of light (VSL) theory' which conjectured that if an engine was built that emitted a light beam a factor longer than that of 'normal' light then it could fly into this beam at several times the speed of light without noticeably increasing its mass. In other words, our Olympic athlete, instead of carrying extra weight, would perform as if he was in a vacuum tube and be sucked along even faster towards his record attempt.

The theory was quickly dismissed by his peers at the time as ridiculous, the maths simply did not work. There were few things in the universe that were constant but as far as they were concerned the speed of light was one them. The last thing scientists wanted to be told was that even this immutable law was in doubt.

George's job was to check everything, so without thinking he quietly reprocessed the calculations in the Portuguese scientist's original paper, replacing where necessary old mathematical techniques with contemporary ones. He then ran the resulting data through his modelling processors that predicted with some accuracy what would happen if the theory was put into practice. Once he had these results, George did something he had never done before; he ignored protocol and woke up Dr. Steel.

Overnight the pair were heralded as heroes, they enjoyed a ticker tape parade in Times Square, Dr. Steel was awarded another Nobel Prize and received an honorary knighthood from King Charles VII of Great Britain. George himself was lauded as being a huge credit to the team, an example of what can be achieved with the correct application. They were invited as guests of honour by many heads of state and for a brief period they were the two most recognisable faces on the planet even appearing on the front page of 'Time

Internet', the most coveted of the electronic newswire services.

Once the fervour had died down it was time for the two scientists to part. Dr. Steel, long past retirement age left Earth for his Martian holiday home, but for George it was not so simple. Unfortunately NASA had no further use for him, he was old, and his memory and processing skills were no longer up to the levels of the younger, newer incumbents. After a short period he was 're-trained', which meant he was sent to their debriefing centre where he was given new skills suitable to his age and then finally re-deployed to a domestic services agency.

George of course did not mind this, whether he was working at the pinnacle of theoretical physics or cleaning up after his master's children, he just wanted to be useful, it did not matter to him. It was just the way he was.

~

Mrs Thomas walked into the dining room and saw George standing there with the duster in his hand,

"Darling." she cried out, "George has stopped again; this is the fourth time this week."

"Ok, I'm coming," replied Mr Thomas, "I'll charge him up again, but maybe you're right, these re-programmed NASA models are long obsolete now, maybe it's time I bought you a 'James' the new Cryson auto-butler".

A Day at the Seaside

Good Prospects

Two brothers in the 1860's worked in their father's grocery store in Southampton. Their positions were secure but they had recognised for some time that the best they could hope for was that one day they would inherit the shop, and life would continue much the same for the rest of their lives.

Then one day, a traveller came back off one of the ships and told them of a huge opportunity in California. Ambitious young men were arriving from all over the world to prospect for gold and some were making a life's fortune in just a few months.

Excited by this opportunity the brothers decided to go to California and chance their arm. The journey was long and arduous taking over six months. When they arrived Frank, the elder of the two couldn't wait to get started. He went straight to the hardware store, bought himself a pick and shovel, staked out a claim for the closest piece of land next to the existing prospectors and got down to work. "Look at all these other guys prospecting, this is where the gold must be." he thought.

He worked hard day and night. He was up at six every morning and worked until it was too dark to see. He dug and he dug. You could not fault his work ethic. He had some success, after the first four weeks he had found enough gold to pay for his board and lodging and he even had a bit of spare cash left over. He was feeling very optimistic. Every Friday he would drink with the other prospectors and they would congratulate each other on how successful they had been. "We are not rich yet, it's a numbers game, if we keep digging we will hit the 'big money' seams."

The other brother Harry, however, did not go straight to hardware store, he didn't buy a pick or a shovel, instead he spent his time talking to the bar owner, the hotel owner, he went on long excursions into the desert, he talked to the old-timers, who had 'seen it all' passing their days outside their lodgings. He even spoke to the clerks in the land registry office. His brother Frank was almost in despair, "What are you doing? we have travelled all this way and so far you have not even *tried* to find any gold."

His brother smiled and replied, "I have been prospecting just as hard as you have."

Finally during the second month, the second brother staked out his claim on a piece of land, which was well away from the other prospectors. He finally bought his pick and shovel and finally he went to work.

He started work at 9 in the morning and finished at 5 in the afternoon. Within three weeks he had found more than three times more gold than his brother had in six weeks. After the first three months, he had found enough gold to employ other men to do the digging. Within a year he had shipped mechanical diggers from the East and was well on the way to owning the largest and most profitable gold mine in California.

Still bemused by his brother's good fortune, the elder brother Frank decided to join the firm. Soon afterwards he finally asked his brother why he had found so much more gold than him, even though he had worked just as hard. His brother replied. "To be successful at prospecting, it is not how long or how often you dig, it's knowing *where* to dig."

A Day at the Seaside

Daisy

Daisy was a young inquisitive cow, different from all the others. She was independent, and single-minded, not for her was a day chewing the cud with the other cows. She liked nothing better than to be off exploring and having adventures in remote parts of the field.

Daisy was also always hungry, she was always looking for new grass to eat, and in every field apart from the one she was in the grass always looked greener.

Daisy lived in a field next to a piece of ground that was too small for grazing and not suitable for crops that had laid fallow for many years. Here lived a well-established community of animals; rabbits, field mice, moles and a family of grass snakes. The community had thrived for years, with many generations living happily and peacefully together in this blissful, quiet sanctuary. The locals called it the 'buttercup field' as it would become a sea of yellow in the summer.

One day Daisy spotted a field in the distance she had never seen before. Her eyes lit up like neon search lights. "Wow." she said, "The grass over there looks so much greener than the grass in my field, I am must go over there and taste it." So, even though the grass in her own field was actually better than the grass in the far field as it had been grown especially with the diet of cows in mind, Daisy struck out to this new promised land stomping directly across the buttercup field.

The result was catastrophic. Homes were crushed, burrows were completely caved in, the children of the field mice were separated from their parents, the grass snake, basking in the sun escaped by literally the 'skin of his teeth'. The residents of the buttercup meadow were very upset, "mindless bloody cow." was one of the more polite cries as they started, slowly, to rebuild their homes. Eventually, normality returned and everyone carried on as before.

Then, six months later it happened again. Daisy, during one of her regular moments of boredom, remembered the thrill she had of visiting the 'green' field across the way. She flushed with excitement and without stopping to think, made a beeline to the verdant pasture. As before, she caused the same devastation, the newly rebuilt homes were crushed once again, and this time the community was up in arms.

"That cow charges about as if she owns the

place, she upsets everyone and leaves without a care in the world." said the vole, "Yes someone needs to have a word with her, before she does any more damage" said the rabbit. "Why don't you go and tell yourself." hissed the grass snake. "Calm down." a voice from the rear whispered. It was the old hare. "I will go and talk to her".

The old hare slowly hopped over to the fence where Daisy was enjoying her fourth breakfast. "Could I have a word Daisy?" asked the old hare. Daisy looked up, upset that she had been disturbed. "What do you want?" she replied rudely. I would like to talk to you about your short-cut across our homes. Twice now you have ploughed across the Buttercup field destroying our homes and habitat. The smaller animals have feared for their lives. You don't seem to care for anyone apart from yourself."

Daisy looked up, and with a bored expression replied, "What Buttercup field?"

Daisy

A Day at the Seaside

Poems and Lyrics

Doors

I am walking down a corridor
It stretches to infinity
It is dark
I feel my way

It is full of doors
Staggered
One to left, one to right
Each one slightly a jar

I walk to a door
I approach, it slams shut
A lock turns
A voice whispers
"This door is not for you."

I walk to another
It slams shut
A lock turns
A voice whispers
"This door is not for you."

I continue walking
Another door slams
Another lock turns
A voice whispers
"This door is not for you."

A bright light appears on the horizon
It comes from a door
I walk past many more doors
They all slam
They all lock
A voice whispers
"These doors are not for you."

The door with the light stays open
It lets me through
I walk into the light
A voice whispers
"This door is for you."

Ice

Born in ancient years
An icy mantle, I am
Balancing creation
A child without fears

Whales whisper in my ear
Bears bask in my garden
Deep the planet breathes
A clean crisp air

I watched the mammoth walk
Beneath my frozen crown
Their feet on solid ground
The Ape had yet to talk

Child of man I now maintain
Home to Inuit innocence
My frosty kingdom shared
Then the Norsemen came

At first the trees were slain
His thirst for power grows
He prays at mammon's altar
I taste a bitter rain

He hunts deep beneath
My cousin's crusty skin
For long dead fossiled friends
Feasting as a thief

As hot as the sun
The engines ignite
A hole to heaven opens
The burning has begun

Borealis's and Orion's belt
Cast their celestial eye
On man's fallacious folly
Watching as I melt

Bleeding pools of icy blood
My wrinkled skin recedes
A watching world weeps
The terrible tears I flood

Stop! My native infants cry
Cease this holocaust
Crack! My fingers fracture
His ears are deaf. I die.

Tomorrow

Tomorrow he will tell her that he has
always loved her
But love is not a commodity that can be traded
over counters
The currency is wondering
The price is misery

The shadow cast is not all it seems
He has the means to realise her dreams
But love can dance many dances
And if you don't pay the piper then the tune
will fade away

Tomorrow he will tell her that he is just an actor
Whose audience is waiting, waiting for a chance
to act in his play
He pretends to have a reticence
that overcomes his confidence
But his ego is as fragile, as fragile as a seashell
and can be shattered by a careless word

The shadow cast is not all it seems
He has the means to realise her dreams
But love can dance many dances
And if you don't pay the piper then the tune
will fade away

Tomorrow he will tell her that love is not
a prisoner
That can be locked away in cages
It has to have its freedom
Or it will fly away

Tomorrow he will tell her that he has
always loved her
But love is not a commodity that can be
traded over counters
The currency is wondering
The price is misery

What is Love?

I don't know what's traditional
For me, my love for you is unconditional
Every time you leave
My heart stops beating and I no longer breathe

My soul aches
For my soul mate
A part of me is amiss
I long for just one kiss

I need something for the pain
It won't stop
Until I see you again

When you are back, I am complete
From my head to my feet
That's what love is!

I wish

I wish
I wish I could drive a ragtop car
I wish I could play right hand guitar
I wish all my lyrics sounded like prose
I wish that you love me, but heaven knows
I wish all my hopes are not just dreams
I wish the truth was more than it seems
I wish that we will always be together
I wish our love would last for ever
I wish

Searching

I have been searching
I know I will find you
You keep on hiding
It's me you are seeking

When you accept this prophecy
You will find your destiny
There is no regret in me
This is not a gift of charity

It may just look like fun
There is no where you can run
You're trapped in a moment
You need to be with someone

Time is not standing still
I think you know the way I feel
Step on the floor, accept the dance
Time to give us a chance

Look

She looks up from her book at a man
He's dressed in a suit, carrying a case
full of loot
he gets all the action he can

He looks up from his book at a girl
She is dressed in a dress, her hair is a mess,
her mind isn't straight it's a whirl

She looks up from her book at a mirror
She's dressed in a skirt, she's desperate to flirt,
but the man in the suit disappears.

Nothing to say

I'm just not myself today
I don't care what you say
You tell me that you love me
And then you go away

I'm going through the motions
I'm mid-way through the play
I'm an actor with a script
But the script has nothing to say

If love is the lead
Then how can I follow
If the chorus is the colour
Then I am the mono
....and your heart is full of hollow.

Woman in a window

Woman in a window
Red light on the door
Man on a business trip
Coming back for more

Woman in a window
Chains around your feet
Offering some comfort
To everyone you meet

I know where I am in Amsterdam
I know where I am in Amsterdam
The lights of the city will catch you if they can

Woman in window
Tears upon your cheek
Looking for a prince
You can never keep

Woman in a window
Red light on the door
You look familiar
Have we met before?

I Know where I am in Amsterdam
The lights of the city will catch you if they can
The De Wallen girls will not make you a man

Woman in a window
Still a daddy's daughter
Open for business
Sold for bricks and mortar

I know where I am in Amsterdam
The De Wallen girls will not make you a man
Don't be the Guilder in another's pension plan

Brief Encounter

Their eyes met for a moment
It happened on platform five
In a tearoom on a station
A moment to change their lives

It takes just a second to fall in love
Like a spell cast from above

Like trains in the night
Their lives were on-track
Though a cloud of emotion
There was no going back

It takes just a second to fall in love
Like a spell cast from above

There are signals in the guardroom
There are signals in the heart
When they are not together
Their lives are torn apart

They both had one way tickets
To a destination unknown
They would pass many stations
But they'd never be alone

For this was their brief encounter
In the carriage made of time
Holding hands together
For few more stops down the line

Fallen Tree

No one can know the places I know
And no one can know where I've been
No one can hear the voices I hear
And no one can know what I've seen

No one can feel the feelings I feel
And no one can know how it feels
No one can see what my eyes can see
And no one has seen me as me

I don't want to be a fallen tree
In a forest that no one can see
I just want us to be you and me
As far as the eye can see

No one has walked the paths that we have walked
A journey that cannot be taught
No one has known the way we feel love
And no one can know how we know

I don't want to be a fallen tree
In a forest that no one can see
I just want us to be you and me
I never want to set you free

No one has stepped into my darkest night
And watched me as I screamed for the light
No one has died, the deaths that I die
And no one ever thought to ask why

I don't want to be a fallen tree
In a forest that no one can see
I just want us to be you and me
Until the end of eternity

Just one look

Even though I wasn't looking
I knew what I had found
Just one look
Turned my life upside down

It's funny when it happens
It's funny but it's true
Not funny like a laugh
But the opposite of blue

I said it couldn't happen
I said it can't be true
But fate chose the moment
To tell me it was you

It's funny when it happens
It's funny but it's true
Not funny like a laugh
But the opposite of blue

I wake up in the morning
Was it something that you said?
I always hear you singing
You are the song inside my head

It's funny when it happens
It's funny but it's true
Not funny like a laugh
But the opposite of blue

Rejected

Wasted years on a dusty shelf
Don't know what I did to myself
Went to take a test, but not selected
No papers, no job, Rejected!

Rejected, silicon chip machines
Rejected, the queen in straight blue jeans
Where do we go from here?
Is the end so near?

Walking down a dirty road
Ignored by most and feeling cold
A hunted species, not protected
No help, no hope, Rejected!

Rejected, silicon chip machines
Rejected, the queen in straight blue jeans
Where do we go from here?
Is the end so near?

A thousand people same as me
Roots at the bottom of society
Like left luggage not collected
Not seen, not heard, Rejected!

Rejected, silicon chip machines
Rejected, the queen in straight blue jeans
Where do we go from here?
Is the end so near?

Fairy Hill

The day is fine
The skies are clear
What to do before a beer
A cycle would be enough
To stretch the legs, not too tough

The chemo legacy was a bitter pill
The muscles, scream, anywhere but Fairy Hill
We set off from home through Keynsham Mill
No one speaks of Fairy Hill

Up Saltford Hill my legs feel the strain
Maybe I should have taken the train
Jane disappears, calling "come on you loser."
"Bollocks to this I'd rather be in the boozer!"

We cruise through the Somerset lanes
Passed Helicopter Hill and the field full of
solar panes

Down past the 'Pig' our wedding place
At thirty miles an hour, we are right on the pace

Closer now we reach the Compton Inn
Drinkers in the garden are making a din
Rounding the corner the brute is in sight
Even from this distance it gives me a fright

I suck in the air and refuse to talk
Got to keep focused, not going to walk
To keep the wheels spinning I drop down a cog
It's mind over matter, I can't see for the fog

Keep it going, keep it going the top is in sight
Heart pumping like crazy and muscles so tight
The top, I've made it, it's easy from here
Just two more miles separate me from a beer

You may have a name that no one could fear
But, you're no fairy, hill.

What the cow thought about the rain

Should I lie down or up should I get

I was never taught the correct etiquette

If I lie down in the grass I cannot eat

And my belly is full when I stand on my feet

If I lie down

Will I catch a cold, or something worse I will
come to regret

Or will I just get wet?

I wonder what a sheep would do

Poems and Lyrics

A Day at the Seaside

About the publisher

Carraway is an independent British publisher based in the West Country.

Named and inspired by the character Nick Carraway in F. Scott Fitzgerald's most famous novel, The Great Gatsby, Carraway was established to make it easy and affordable for talented writers to get their books into print.

Specialising primarily in books covering fiction, travel, business, wellbeing, music, philosophy and biography, Carraway is an ideal starting point for new writers and established authors who are looking for a publisher that offers a more personalised level of attention and support.

For further information visit www.carrawaypublishing.co.uk